EVERGLADES

EVERGLADES

BUFFALO TIGER
AND THE RIVER OF GRASS

PETER LOURIE

BOYDS MILLS PRESS

Published by Caroline House
Boyds Mills Press, Inc.
A Highlights Company
815 Church Street
Honesdale, Pennsylvania 18431
Printed in Mexico

Publisher Cataloging-in-Publication Data
Lourie, Peter.
    Everglades / Buffalo Tiger and the river of grass ;
Peter Lourie.—1st ed.
[48]p. : col. ill. ; cm.
Includes maps.
Summary : An informative text of a trip into the Everglades, complemented by photographs.
ISBN 1-878093-91-6
1. Everglades (Fla.)—Juvenile literature. [1. Everglades (Fla.).]
I. Title.
574.5—dc20   1994
Library of Congress Catalog Card Number 92-73989

First edition, 1994
Book designed by Abby Kagan
The text of this book is set in 13-point New Baskerville.
Distributed by St. Martin's Press

10 9 8 7 6 5 4 3 2 1

Many thanks to the council of the Miccosukee tribe of Indians of Florida: Billy Cypress, Jasper Nelson, Jimmie Bert, Max Billie, and Henry Bert. In addition, a special thanks to Steven Tiger and Marjory Stoneman Douglas.

By Peter Lourie
For young readers:

AMAZON
A Young Reader's Look at the Last Frontier

HUDSON RIVER
An Adventure from the Mountains to the Sea

YUKON RIVER
An Adventure to the Gold Fields of the Klondike

EVERGLADES
Buffalo Tiger and the River of Grass

For adults:

SWEAT OF THE SUN, TEARS OF THE MOON:
A Chronicle of an Incan Treasure

For Buffalo Tiger and Jean Craighead George

CONTENTS

THE RIVER OF GRASS

In the early sixteenth century the Spanish explorer Ponce de León searched the coast of Florida for the Fountain of Youth. He never discovered the mythical fountain, but if he had penetrated deeper into the peninsula that the Spaniards called "the land of flowers," he might have found something else: the Everglades, a slow-moving swamp that is in fact a huge, silent river.

The Everglades, called *Pa-hay-okee*, or "Grassy Water," by the Miccosukee Indians, is often only inches deep, yet it runs a hundred miles from Florida's Lake Okeechobee to the Gulf of Mexico and Florida Bay. In places it is seventy miles wide. It has been called a river of grass because of the dense waves of tawny sawgrass arcing gently to the south, pointing in the direction of the sluggish flow of the water.

The Miccosukee Indians have lived in the Everglades for more than a hundred years. When they first arrived they found the river of grass to be a kind of paradise. Even today, the Grassy Water dazzles the eye with its abundance of birds and other wildlife. Yet, unlike a hundred years ago, there is sadness in this bright spot on the planet. Great pressures from pollution and over-development threaten to destroy the river of grass.

To learn more about the Everglades, I would need a guide who could lead me safely into the sawgrass. It is nothing like ordinary grass. It is a razor-sharp, saw-toothed grass, ten to fifteen feet tall, that can cut human flesh like a knife. There are stories of hunters getting lost in the sawgrass, never to return to camp. Other dangers in the Glades include alligators, deadly snakes like the water moccasin, and an oozing muck called quicksand that can bury a person alive. Finding an experienced guide to lead me into the Everglades seemed like the only wise thing to do.

1

BUFFALO TIGER

I had heard of a Miccosukee Indian named Buffalo Tiger who knew the Everglades from his boyhood days. And to find him I drove west on the road that runs across Florida cutting the Everglades in two. Constructed between 1926 and 1928, this road is called the Tamiami Trail because it joins Tampa on the west coast of Florida to Miami on the east coast.

At the Miccosukee Reservation, forty miles west of Miami, I found Mr. Tiger, who had been chief of his tribe for thirty-three years. Now retired, he runs a small airboat service for tourists. He agreed to teach me as much as I could learn about the Everglades.

In days past, perhaps sixty years ago, Buffalo Tiger's family had lived by hunting and fishing. It had been a peaceful existence, and then the white people came and changed everything.

Buffalo Tiger

Now the tribe survives by making crafts, wrestling alligators to entertain tourists, and taking visitors into the Glades in airboats. To me, Buffalo did not seem angry about the changes, although I gradually found out that he had much to be angry about.

Buffalo Tiger is not his Indian name but the name he uses in the white man's world. When he was a boy, he was a powerful runner. Everyone said he ran like a buffalo. His true Indian name remains a Miccosukee secret. When Buffalo Tiger turned fourteen, he passed a tribal test of manhood at the annual initiation ceremony, which takes place at the Green Corn Dance, held in the late spring. The location of the dance is known only to the Miccosukees. He spent a whole day and night without sleep or food, preparing for the ceremony. Afterward he was given a Miccosukee man's name that would be his for the rest of his life.

The day I first visited Buffalo, it was another hot, dry afternoon of a long drought. There had been little rain for years, and the sawgrass had turned a deeper brown than usual. Soon Buffalo might have to stop running his airboats because lower water meant too much mud. If it didn't rain soon, fires might destroy sawgrass everywhere, as had happened a few years back.

The ecology of the Everglades seems to have been permanently altered by human interference. Southern Florida has experienced booming development for the

This image of Miami, Florida, is from a Landsat 5 satellite orbiting 438 miles above the earth. This is not a photograph. It is a special kind of computer image that combines infrared and visible light. By looking at the colors, scientists can see the sharp contrast between developed and undeveloped areas. Healthy vegetation appears in shades of red. Vegetation in different stages of growth is seen as oranges and yellows. Different soils are shown as green and brown. Urban areas are white, blue, and gray. Deep water is very dark blue and black.

The Everglades is the large area in the left half of the image. Sawgrass makes up most of the Glades. It can be seen in shades of red, depending on its health and the amount of moisture it contains. The oblong orange specks are small islands called hammocks. They are covered with shrubs and trees such as palm, pine, oak, and cypress.

If you look at the shape of the Everglades, you can see something very important. The entire marshland is arching toward the city because so much water is being drained away.

past century. Miami, one of the state's principal cities, keeps expanding to the west, eating up the Glades. Today hundreds of people move to Florida each week. This migration has greatly strained the supply of drinking water in the region. Agriculture also has had an impact on the Everglades. Farms and sugar plantations use the water from Lake Okeechobee and pollute it with pesticides. Over the years the U.S. Army Corps of Engineers has built dams and dikes to regulate the water flow of the Glades. The natural processes of the river have been overcontrolled, and the spontaneous, gradual flow of water from Okeechobee to the Gulf has been hindered. Some believe that such tampering with the complex ecosystem of the Glades may have resulted in years of drought and altered weather patterns.

When Buffalo Tiger was a boy, the water in the Everglades was bright and clear, and the region was filled with natural wonders. Buffalo remembers gazing from his canoe at small shiny fish flashing like silk in the sunlight as they broke the surface of the water. Today the wildlife in the Everglades is threatened as never before. People have overhunted the alligators for their hides and the birds for their plumes. There is, however, a growing movement among environmentalists to return the river of grass to its natural state, even though some fear it might be too late.

The Miccosukees did not always live in the Everglades. They once lived in the north of Florida, but white farmers stole their rich farmland and burned their houses and crops. The Miccosukees tried to fight back but were outnumbered. They fled south in the 1820s.

In 1830 the federal government set aside land in Oklahoma and Arkansas for the Miccosukees and tried to force them onto these reservations. Formerly a

A Miccosukee settlement in the Glades (early 1920s)

The Tiger family (early 1920s)

peaceful tribe, the Miccosukees grew angry. For decades they moved deeper into the Everglades and fought battles against soldiers who tried to capture them. They found a perfect hiding place in the Grassy Water. They became so familiar with the swampy terrain that they could outsmart the white men, who floundered in the muck. They hid from the soldiers in the sawgrass. They lay unseen in the mud, and they camped on the nearly invisible islands, called hammocks, deep in the Glades. In order to avoid detection, they scattered onto many of these hammocks, a few families per island. They even used certain kinds of "smokeless" wood for their fires so they would not be seen from far away. They learned to hunt and fish in the Glades. They ate turtles and venison, and they planted beans, squash, and bananas. And from the few remaining Calusa Indians, who had lived in the Everglades for centuries but who had been all but exterminated by the Europeans, they learned how to make open-air thatch huts they called *chi-kees*.

So successful were the Miccosukees in adapting to life in the Glades that when Buffalo was a boy he knew very little about white people. The Miccosukees continued to keep away from the whites who were coming in ever-greater numbers. Buffalo Tiger remembers how he and his friends would lie in the grass watching them, but they never mixed with the white boys. Buffalo didn't play with a white boy until he was fourteen.

But in the late 1940s and early 1950s more and more of the tribe emerged from hiding. They could no longer survive in the changing Everglades. Wildlife was scarce, and it was increasingly difficult to find food.

Today most Miccosukees live along the highway on the Miccosukee Reservation, some in modern homes, and others in the traditional Miccosukee *chi-kees.* Like some Miccosukees, however, Buffalo has chosen not to live on the reservation anymore. He has a home in Miami. So much has changed in a short time.

Miccosukee children (early 1920s)

When Buffalo Tiger was twelve, he practiced the Miccosukee philosophy of taking only what he needed from the Everglades, and no more. He hunted only the fish and game that his family needed to survive. As is true of other Native American groups, the Miccosukees do not believe in owning land. They believe that they exist to protect the land and to keep it healthy so their tribe may flourish. Surely they lament the day the white people came to the Everglades, when so many alligators were killed for skins and so many frogs for food, and the Miccosukee land was stolen and divided by those who believed in owning land. The whites built canals and drained the Everglades for farming. Today the land is seriously ill. It no longer supplies food for the tribe.

In 1947 the federal government established the Everglades National Park and moved the Miccosukees off more than two million acres. The Miccosukees became stewards of a mere 76,000 acres. And the Miccosukees began to work for white people in order to survive in their new life along the road.

Buffalo Tiger was perhaps the first of his tribe in this century to lead the Miccosukees toward self-reliance. In 1952 he was appointed chief, or spokesperson, for the Miccosukees, and he retired thirty-three years later, in 1985. Buffalo believed that the tribe's survival depended on learning the ways of the white people so that the Miccosukees could organize effectively against the white invaders. Buffalo traveled around the world studying how other native groups had organized themselves. In 1961 the tribe, under the direction of Buffalo, was given control of its own political affairs by the United States government. This has helped somewhat. But even so, the tribe has lost more than it has gained.

The Miccosukees made these canoes from large cypress trees (early 1920s).

2

INTO THE EVERGLADES

The day came when I would enter the Everglades by airboat. Buffalo's assistant canoed out and disappeared among the reeds. Suddenly there was a loud roar, like the sound of an airplane revving up. From behind the bushes, where it had been anchored for safety from vandals, the big airboat moved cautiously up to the dock. And what an odd contraption this airboat was: part airplane, part boat. It reminded me of a go-cart I had built as a boy, though it was much bigger. The propeller was driven by an engine so noisy, Buffalo Tiger had to put hearing protectors over his ears. Buffalo stepped up to the controls and sat high above the water, where he could see over the sawgrass. He steered with a long stick in one hand. From his high seat he could look out at the channels and find the best route through the Glades.

Scouting a route through the Glades

Off we roared, frightening birds by the hundreds. The boat skimmed over the mud and through the tall grass as if it might take off. It seemed hardly to touch the water. Later, Buffalo told me that driving an airboat isn't as simple as it looks. Even an airboat can get tangled in sawgrass and mud.

Airboats are recent arrivals to the Glades. When Buffalo was a boy, he and his friends poled heavy dugout canoes made from large cypress trees. But now most of the big trees have been cut, and the remaining ones grow on private property. So there are no more dugouts, though Buffalo told me he would love to get his hands on a cypress to build another canoe.

We headed out into the Glades at top speed, following the airboat trails, which look like canals cut in the sawgrass. The 360-degree expanse of blue sky made me dizzy. Suddenly the engine died, and we sat out there alone. The wind raked through the high sawgrass. Buffalo pointed to some trees on the horizon.

"I was born right over there," he said. "Our family had six islands, what we call hammocks. We built our homes on one big hammock, which was high enough to be protected even in a hurricane. We used the other islands for farming."

The islands he was talking about were difficult for me to see. It took a practiced eye to locate them.

The trees in the distance mark a hammock.

Airboat trails look like canals in the sawgrass.

Buffalo had recently cleared a field and built Miccosukee-style homes, the traditional palm-thatch *chikees,* on a nearby hammock. Someday, he said, he would take me to that favorite hammock of his.

"Could I camp there?" I asked, though I was afraid he would say no.

"Perhaps one of these days, if we become friends," he said. Then he put on his ear protectors and started the engine, and away we fled over the golden grass beneath the navy blue sky. I felt free out there, the way I often feel at sea when there is nothing in sight but water.

We came shushing to a halt again. We were sitting in a patch of mud beside a wall of ten-foot-high sawgrass. I ran my hand down a blade of grass. It was three-sided and had "teeth." Buffalo pointed to the mud, explaining that alligators and snakes like to go underneath it because it is cool down there. Buffalo grabbed a long pole and poked it over the side into the mud, which he called quicksand. He told me about the danger of quicksand. If I should ever get caught in this mud, he said, I should lie down immediately and crawl the way alligators do on their bellies.

"There's a mother alligator in here right now," he said, "with her young." Buffalo poked the mud with his pole and started to call her out with a kind of croaking sound in his throat, an alligator mating call! The mother alligator finally rose to the surface begrudgingly and slid over the mud. She came to rest watching us.

*An alligator rose out
of the mud.*

"When I was a boy out here," said Buffalo, "the alligators didn't seem so mean. But I think with all the changes and the hunting now, they are getting meaner." Buffalo's face was stern. The airboat roared into action.

A blue heron and an egret flew into the horizon. The wind seemed everpresent, the way it does in a desert. We raced home in the dusk while the water lilies closed up for the night. I wondered how Buffalo and the other Miccosukees had hidden from the white men for so many years. Then I remembered that those were the days before the airboats, when the whites would have to slog through the Glades by foot or pole their boats in a swamp they knew little about.

I hoped to get to his hammock soon.

There still had been no rain, and Buffalo wasn't sure we could get to his island, but we'd try. Today, he said, we would bring three Miccosukee boys with us. Unlike Buffalo and his generation, these young Miccosukees had never lived in the Glades. Buffalo was concerned that the boys watched too much television for entertainment. When he was a boy, he said, he had found many fascinating entertainments in the Glades. He would watch the fish or call to the birds, and he would hide in the bushes watching them flock to the trees by the hundreds. Or, at dusk, when the birds gathered in one tree to sleep, he and his friends might sit below the tree and catch a few.

Buffalo Tiger worries that the younger generation of Miccosukees might be forgetting their heritage. So two days a week he teaches children the old ways.

An aerial view of Buffalo Tiger's hammock

He is also writing down what he learned from his boyhood years living in the Glades. He hopes to pass this knowledge to the younger generation. "I do think Indian children have to find the good things in themselves about being Indian," he told me. "We were here for a long time before the whites came. We did not destroy the Everglades, nor should we destroy ourselves or forget our Indian culture."

Aboard the airboat

The three Miccosukee boys arrived in their mothers' cars. Jack Wilson, Joshua Osceola, and Ryan Billie seemed cautious, a bit timid, yet proud and confident, too. Perhaps they were wary of me, a white man. Actually, this would be their first visit to Buffalo's island, and I could tell that beneath their cool exterior, they were as excited as I was. On the way to the island the boys sat quietly as the wind whipped their black hair about their faces.

The small hammock appeared from nowhere. Suddenly the boat was coming up to dry land. Open-sided huts with palmetto roofs appeared from behind brambles. Buffalo said the island was called Tear Island. The story goes that many years ago two Miccosukee men had wanted this island for themselves, but it was too small and could not support two families. The man who lost the island shed many tears.

On this tiny hammock, Buffalo had built a camp of *chi-kees*. These were replicas of the homes he grew up in before his tribe moved out of the Everglades proper and over to the Tamiami Trail. The Miccosukee *chi-kee* is square with open sides so the breezes can blow through it. Four cypress poles are driven into the ground. And a floor of logs sits three feet off the ground to protect the family from snakes and floods. The palmetto palm fronds that form the roof drape over the sides to keep the rain out during storms.

The women prepare meals in the "cooking *chi-kee*," but the family maintains a separate "living *chi-kee*," where the food is brought after it is prepared. In the "sleeping *chi-kee*" the night's bedding is stored in the rafters to allow the women room to work during the day.

The boys gather under a cooking chi-kee.

The boys build a fire.

Typically, the Miccosukee family would have one or two additional islands nearby to farm. There they would plant corn, potatoes, pumpkins, tomatoes, beans, bananas, and sugar cane. When Buffalo was a boy, he used to come to Tear Island for certain fruits, like the custard apple. It was a place where he and his friends would play, too.

When we got out of the boat, Buffalo gave the boys some orders in the Miccosukee language, which sounded beautiful out there in the wild. They scattered to find dry wood for a fire. Buffalo had the boys build the fire in the traditional way, with the logs pointing to the four corners of the earth. The wind talked in the big pine tree by the water, where Buffalo had pulled the boat to the dock. A torn Miccosukee flag flapped forlornly. The tribal flag has four bands of color: yellow, red, black, and white. Yellow represents the east, where the sun rises and life begins. Red is for the north, which represents the middle of life, and black is for the west, where Miccosukees go when they die. White stands for the south and the return of the sun and the renewal of life. These colors represent the whole universe spinning in a circle, what the Miccosukees consider the Circle of Life.

The boys scoured the island for burnable wood. Buffalo had taught them which wood burns best. Among the Miccosukees it is traditionally the uncle who teaches the boys. Buffalo's uncle had shown him how to build a *chi-kee* and gather firewood and certain plants and fruits for the women to cook.

"You see, Peter, a little Miccosukee boy becomes a man very early. He learns by listening to his uncle, and he learns by doing the practical jobs of farming and hunting. We always listened with great respect to our elders. Not so today. I see boys and girls not listening. This is something we would never have done."

After the fire had been lit in Buffalo's cooking *chi-kee,* the boys settled down to listen to Buffalo tell tales of the old days. He repeated stories they knew about the Breathmaker.

The Breathmaker is the Miccosukees' God. According to the teachings of the Breathmaker, the whole world was underwater at one time. Then the water drained off, and the land was open. All the animals and people were free to wander wherever they chose. The Breathmaker taught the Miccosukees to care for the land and the animals, which they depended upon.

Buffalo reminded the boys of many things. He told them that Miccosukee medicine men, the priests who help people live by the laws of the Breathmaker, are the spiritual leaders of the tribe even today. One of the laws says that the earth turns in a circle of life, beginning in the east, moving north, then around to the west, and finally down to the south, and back east again. The tribal fire, which might burn for months before going out, must always be laid with the logs pointing in the four

Buffalo shares stories with his young friends.

directions. All the logs meet in the center. The first log points east, and the rest follow in the same circle of life.

Miccosukees were brought up to live in harmony with nature, he said. Animals and birds were like their brothers and sisters. Children were taught to respect all living things. People understood their place in nature, and nature in turn treated the tribe well.

The Miccosukee religion depends today as much as in the past on loyalty to family. Families are grouped into clans, such as the Panther, Otter, Wind, Snake, and Bird clans. There is even a Big City Clan. The separate clans have their own rules and responsibilities. Buffalo Tiger is a member of the Bird Clan, famous for making war and peace and for being good speakers. Buffalo is a natural storyteller. He learned many of his stories from his clan. These stories, which often contain a moral, were his schooling.

Every clan provides for the tribe as a whole. And a member of one clan must go outside of his or her clan to marry. Boys become members of their mother's clan. This is why it is their uncle, their mother's brother, who teaches them the laws of both the clan and the tribe. Buffalo's uncle taught him to be a good hunter, to help the family, to behave, and to be strong.

"Yes, I can remember the feeling of freedom," Buffalo said to the boys. "When I was your age I loved to harvest the wild sugar cane. I loved to chew it. Moving from one island to the other in a canoe with my friends was the best feeling of all. I remember listening carefully to the wind. As a boy I learned about the wind and the trees, the rain and the lightning, the water, the moon, and the stars. We could tell what would happen to the weather just by looking at the sky and feeling the wind. I used to love storms, even when I was very young. The wild rain would whip up the Everglades and I would run and jump. Once I got so excited I shot my toy arrow into the air and it came down on my grandfather's head."

When Buffalo finished telling stories, Ryan, Joshua, and Jack plowed into the surrounding bushes to explore the island some more. After a while, Buffalo said it was time to go. I asked if I could camp on Tear Island on my next trip. I was surprised and happy when Buffalo said yes.

Buffalo poured water on the fire, and we all hopped into the airboat and headed into the sawgrass.

When we got back to the road, Ryan Billie asked me if I really planned to spend the night alone on that island. All three boys seemed shocked by the idea. Ryan wondered whether I had seen the ghost's house on the island. "What ghost's house?" I wanted to know. "The little ghost's house on the branch," he said. "The thing that looked like a cocoon of cobwebs. The whole reservation is haunted by those ghosts." The boys believed that if I should disturb that little ghost house, I would be in big trouble.

Leaving the hammock

CHAPTER
4

THROUGH THE NIGHT

By the time I saw Buffalo a few months later, it had finally rained. For two weeks it had rained every day, and the water was rising in the sawgrass. Buffalo was happy because his airboats would do a better business with the tourists. He said, "So, you are ready to spend the night on my island, eh?"

I thought I was ready, although I can't deny that I felt some fear. But spending a night alone on Buffalo's island seemed like the best way to experience the Everglades that Buffalo had known as a boy. I wanted to feel the wind in the night, with no one around. There would be no airboat to help me get off the island if I ran into difficulty. It was a challenge. Like all challenges, however, this one came with a certain amount of fear. But what was I afraid of? Was it that I would be alone on an island with no way off? Was it ghosts?

When we reached Tear Island, the wind was stronger than ever. I looked for the tiny ghost house Ryan had told me about but did not find it. Maybe it had blown away.

Buffalo helped me build a fire in the Miccosukee manner. He said the smoke would keep the mosquitoes away. Then we walked around the island, and he showed me a wild papaya tree and a tree from which the Miccosukees had made bows and arrows. Members of his clan had once lived on the island, perhaps as long as sixty years ago. I asked if he ever thought about living out here again.

"I don't know. Maybe someday. I love it here. I like to come here to get away from the cars. But I haven't lived on a hammock in many years. I'd have to get used to it again. And the water is no good anymore. Can't drink it! Too many pesticides."

Building a fire

Gathering pond apples

Before Buffalo left me alone on the island, he said, "So let me know what you see and hear. There are wildcats, raccoons, and owls out here. But, Peter, be careful where you step. There are two snakes that can kill you, the water moccasin and the diamondback rattle-snake. So look carefully before you pick up a piece of wood. And watch where you put your hands and feet."

The apprehension I felt about this camping trip grew into a moment of terror as Buffalo jumped onto his airboat perch, waved good-bye, pulled his bright orange protectors over his ears, and started up the engine. Reluctantly, I pushed his boat out into the water.

As he steered the airboat away from the island, the wind from the propeller nearly knocked me over. The boat disappeared, its engine growing fainter and fainter until the wind rushed in to take its place entirely. And I was alone.

The first thing I did was set up my tent while a curious egret walked around the camp. After I explored the island, I returned to cook my dinner. The mos-quitoes appeared, and I slapped the little insects, feeling twinges of fear. I realized that my only way off Tear Island would be a mad dash through the sawgrass and the quicksand, which Buffalo had discouraged me from doing.

I watched the light go slanted and golden, then lavender just before darkness. The wind sang a lonely song in the big pine tree. The moon rose almost full.

I pitched my tent at sunset.

Night is a time for spirits, say the Miccosukees. At dusk the friendly spirit of the day dies. The Miccosukee children learn to respect and fear the night and are taught not to fall asleep at twilight for fear of losing their life, for a life can slip so easily into the fading evening. All Miccosukees are taught to sleep with their heads facing east toward the sunrise of the next day, which will bring new life.

When the mosquitoes multiplied, I dove for my tent. I put my head toward the east just as the Miccosukees do. I imagined the spirits of the darkness roaming about. When Buffalo was very young, he thought he saw a ghost. A strange light appeared at the foot of his bed in the shape of a big ax. It just hung in the air, and then it moved back and forth before it vanished. He did not scream. He woke his mother. His parents got the medicine man to help get rid of the bad spirit.

Suddenly I heard the sound of an airboat coming closer in the darkness. Buffalo had warned me to watch out for hunters. The engine stopped. The boat seemed very close to the island. I wondered if the hunters, who look for alligators with flashlights, would come for me, too. But then the boat moved away.

As I lay in my tent remembering all that Buffalo had told me, a bug crawled over my face. I squashed it and then felt guilty. The Miccosukees believe that people should not harm anything small, because one day something big might harm them.

The Miccosukees respect the night.

The Everglades, growing loud with night birds and bullfrogs, was coming alive in the moonlit night. There was rustling down by the water. I stepped out of my tent to shine my flashlight. I heard a raucous screech from the big pine tree that sent me stumbling backward. But I saw only some silvery wings disappearing into the black sky.

Later I thought I saw a flash of light in the forest, and I wondered if someone else could be living on another part of the island. Then I heard a distinct moaning coming from the water. I remembered that Buffalo had told me that when alligators are really hungry they will eat mud.

Fireflies by the zillion swooped under the *chi-kees* and all around the tent. And I was asleep.

In the morning I wandered around the island, doing what Buffalo had done as a child. I took time to observe. I looked into the weeds. I found a purple gallinule, a small water bird with long thin feet and a red bill. I saw a raccoon in the wild papaya tree. I searched in the water along shore for the same shiny fish that Buffalo saw as a child. But the water was too murky to see anything much. Then I heard an airboat a long

A beautiful water bird, called a purple gallinule, and a curious raccoon in a papaya tree were my animal companions on the hammock.

distance away, and I hoped it would be Buffalo Tiger. As the roar grew louder, though, I began to miss the silence and the solitude.

Buffalo was smiling at me from way up on his airboat perch. It was already ten in the morning, and he'd brought me a cup of coffee. After the engine went dead, he asked, "Did you hear any owls last night? Did you see any ghosts?" I told him about the screech in the pine. He said it was certainly an owl.

It was hard to leave that island without feeling a little sad, for it seemed to represent a Miccosukee way of life that is pretty much forgotten. My night on Buffalo's island gave me a new respect for the Everglades and the people who had lived there for so long.

Back on the road, I sat with Buffalo one last time before I drove away. I looked at the old chief, feeling that I could see him better now than ever before. Buffalo is unique among his tribespeople. He has mixed with the white world more than most Miccosukees. It must be very hard for any Miccosukee to live in both the Indian world and the white world and to maintain the old tribal beliefs.

Like the rest of his tribe, Buffalo grew up with stories about the evils of the white man. Somehow Buffalo didn't believe all of them and he does not hate the white man. Perhaps that is why he made such a good chief and accomplished so much for the tribe.

I was glad he had accepted me and given me his time. He had proved to be a generous teacher. Surely he had taught me only a fraction of what he knows about the Everglades, but in doing so he had shared with me his gift of openness. He had shared his culture with someone from a very different world. I learned that if you believe something strongly, you can remain strong, even when the world tries to weaken you, as the white man's world has tried to weaken the Miccosukee world.

Buffalo Tiger and his tribe have lost their paradise in the Grassy Water. They have lost the Everglades to pollution and agriculture and overdevelopment. But Buffalo remains strong because of what he learned from his tribe when he was a boy. If we are to save the Everglades from further destruction, we must listen to the Miccosukees. The Breathmaker taught them to protect the earth, the birds, and the animals. The Breathmaker taught them to take only what they need, and no more.

A Miccosukee mother and her children (early 1920s)

Author's note:

Many people group the Miccosukees with the Seminole tribe, which has a similar ancestry. In my text, however, I have distinguished the Miccosukee Indians as a separate tribe, for this is the way Buffalo Tiger and the Miccosukees prefer to see themselves.

Also, this book was written a few months before Hurricane Andrew blew through the Glades, leaving widespread destruction. The big tree on Tear Island came down as did many of the larger trees in the Glades. The houses of the Miccosukees along the Tamiami Trail took a beating. Buffalo's *chi-kees* lost their roofs, and his airboats were found loose in the sawgrass, dented but in working condition. Buffalo assured me that the Glades would recover from this natural disaster, the way the River of Grass has always recovered from hurricanes.